The Armanis

The Hero Within

Jayat Ganguly

ISBN 978-93-5883-067-5
© Jayat Ganguly 2023

Published in India 2023 by Pencil

A brand of
One Point Six Technologies Pvt. Ltd.
Unit no. 26, Ground Floor, Building A1,
Wadala Truck Terminal Road,
Near Post Office, Antop Hill, Mumbai - 400037
E connect@thepencilapp.com
W www.thepencilapp.com

DISCLAIMER: *This is a work of fiction. Names, characters, places, events and incidents are the products of the author's imagination. The opinions expressed in this book do not seek to reflect the views of the Publisher.*

Author biography

Jayat Ganguly is a bestselling author known for his gripping and thought-provoking novels. Born and raised in a small town, Jayat developed a deep love for storytelling and the power of words from an early age. His vivid imagination and passion for literature led him to pursue a career as a writer.

Jayat's journey as an author began with his debut novel - "Back from Hell", which quickly garnered critical acclaim and a dedicated following of readers. Since then, he has continued to captivate audiences with his compelling storytelling and well-crafted characters. With each new book, Jayat delves into different genres, showcasing his versatility and mastery of storytelling techniques.

His works often explore complex themes such as love, loss, identity, and the human condition, prompting readers to contemplate life's deeper questions. Whether it's a suspenseful thriller, a poignant family drama, or a captivating historical fiction, Jayat's novels are known for their ability to resonate with readers on an emotional level.

Jayat's writing style is characterized by its evocative prose, meticulous attention to detail, and skillful pacing that keeps readers on the edge of their seats. His ability to create immersive worlds and multidimensional characters has earned him a loyal fan base and numerous literary accolades.

When he's not writing, Jayat enjoys spending time outdoors, drawing inspiration from nature for his storytelling. He also actively engages with his readers through book signings, literary events, and social media, valuing the connection and feedback from his dedicated fans.

With each new project, Jayat Ganguly continues to push the boundaries of his craft, captivating readers and solidifying his place as one of the most talented and influential authors of his generation.

CONTENTS

Foreword

Dear Children,

Welcome to the enchanting world of "The Armanis". As you turn the pages of this delightful book, you are about to embark on a remarkable journey filled with magic, adventure, and heartwarming stories.

Children's books have a unique ability to captivate young minds, ignite their imaginations, and instill valuable life lessons. They transport us to extraordinary places, introduce us to unforgettable characters, and inspire us to dream big. Jayat Ganguly, the brilliant author of this book, has masterfully crafted a collection of stories that will do just that.

In the following pages, you will meet brave heroes and heroines who discover the power of friendship, resilience, and kindness. You will encounter whimsical creatures, explore imaginary worlds, and learn important lessons about empathy, acceptance, and the beauty of being true to oneself.

Jayat Ganguly's storytelling prowess shines through as they weave tales that will make you laugh, gasp, and perhaps shed a tear or two. They have created a cast of characters that will capture your hearts and stay with you long after you've finished reading.

But this book is not just meant to entertain; it is meant to inspire. Within these stories, you will find messages that encourage you to believe in yourself, follow your dreams, and embrace the incredible potential that lies within you. Each story is a gentle reminder that, no matter how small you may feel, you possess the power to make a difference in the world.

As you journey through these pages, I encourage you to let your imagination run wild. Picture yourself alongside the characters, explore the vibrant landscapes, and let the stories come alive in your mind. Remember, the magic of a book lies in your ability to fully immerse yourself in its pages and create a world that is uniquely your own.

So, dear readers, get ready to set sail on this extraordinary adventure. Let the stories within this book transport you to places where anything is possible, where dreams come true, and where the power of imagination knows no bounds.

Enjoy every moment, cherish every word, and let the stories in this book ignite the spark of wonder and imagination that resides within you.

Happy reading!

AG

Preface

Writing short stories for children is an absolute joy and a privilege. It is within the realm of children's literature that we have the opportunity to nurture young minds, ignite their imaginations, and instill lifelong values. The impact of these stories can shape a child's perspective, foster their creativity, and leave an indelible mark on their hearts.

In crafting these stories, I have endeavored to create a collection that celebrates the imagination, embraces diversity, and imparts important life lessons. Through relatable characters and relatable situations, I hope to inspire children to dream big, overcome obstacles, and cherish heroes. Each tale is a small gift, waiting to be unwrapped and treasured by young minds.

As a writer for children, I understand the responsibility that comes with the task. It is not only about entertaining but also about providing a safe space for exploration, discovery, and growth. Children are the future, and it is our duty to empower them with stories that encourage empathy, kindness, and the pursuit of knowledge.

I firmly believe that the world of children's literature is a place where boundaries can be pushed, imagination can soar, and dreams can come true. It is my hope that these stories will transport children to extraordinary worlds, spark their creativity, and inspire them to become the heroes of their own stories.

To the young readers who will embark on these literary journeys, I invite you to open your hearts and minds, to embrace the magic that lies within these pages. May these stories become your companions, your sources of laughter, and your windows to the endless possibilities that await you.

With utmost gratitude and excitement, I present to you this collection of short stories, hoping that they will touch your lives, ignite your imaginations, and accompany you on countless adventures.

Warmest Regards,

Jayat Ganguly

Acknowledgements

Writing a book is not a solitary endeavor; it is the culmination of the support, encouragement, and contributions of numerous individuals. I would like to express my deepest gratitude to those who have been instrumental in bringing this book to life.

First and foremost, I would like to thank my family and Renoo maam for their unwavering love, understanding, and belief in my passion for writing. Your constant support has been a guiding light throughout this creative journey.

To my friends and fellow writers, thank you for your invaluable feedback, brainstorming sessions, and words of encouragement. Your insights and perspectives have enriched the storytelling process and helped me grow as a writer.

Lastly, but certainly not least, I want to express my deepest appreciation to the readers—children and their families—who have embraced my stories with open hearts and minds. Your enthusiasm and support are what motivates me to continue writing and sharing my imagination with the world.

Writing this book has been an incredible journey, and I am humbled by the love and support that have surrounded me throughout. To each and every person who has contributed to this project in any way, thank you from the

bottom of my heart.
With heartfelt gratitude,
Jayat Ganguly

Introduction

To all the wonderful children of the world,

This book is lovingly dedicated to you. You are the brightest stars in our universe, the embodiment of curiosity, imagination, and boundless potential. It is in your eyes that the magic of storytelling truly comes alive.

May these pages ignite your imagination, transport you to extraordinary worlds, and inspire you to dream big. Each word is a whisper from my heart, hoping to bring joy, wonder, and valuable lessons to your lives.

You are the heroes and heroines of your own stories, capable of achieving great things and making a positive impact on the world. Embrace your uniqueness, nurture your dreams, and always remember that you have the power to create a better tomorrow.

May this book be a cherished companion on your journey, a portal to new adventures, and a source of inspiration and comfort. Share it with friends and loved ones, and let its stories and lessons be a source of laughter, reflection, and growth.

Thank you for being the brightest stars in my universe. It is an honor and a joy to share these stories with you. May they spark your imagination, warm your heart, and remind you of the boundless magic that resides within each and every one of you.

With love and gratitude,
Jayat Ganguly

Major Arjun Singh

Major Arjun Singh of the Indian Army was known for his bravery and strong sense of duty. He had always been a fearless and selfless individual, and it was this unwavering commitment that had earned him the admiration and respect of his fellow officers.

One fateful day, during a routine military exercise near the border, disaster struck. A group of officers, including Major Arjun's close friend, Captain Vikram Singh, found themselves caught in a dangerous ambush set up by a notorious terrorist outfit. The officers were outnumbered and outgunned, their lives hanging precariously in the balance.

News of the ambush reached the Indian Army headquarters, causing a stir among the entire unit. Major Arjun, upon hearing about the dire situation his comrades were in, wasted no time in formulating a rescue plan. He knew time was of the essence, and any delay could cost his fellow officers their lives.

Gathering a team of skilled soldiers who shared his sense of urgency, Major Arjun led the charge towards the ambush site. The journey was arduous, with treacherous terrain and dangerous enemy forces blocking their way.

But Major Arjun's spirit remained unyielding.

Finally arriving at the ambush location, Major Arjun assessed the situation before devising a strategic plan. With precision and calm, he executed a series of well-coordinated maneuvers that destabilized the enemy's defenses and turned the tide in their favor.

Under Major Arjun's leadership, the soldiers pushed forward relentlessly, rescuing their trapped comrades one by one. Amidst the chaos of battle, Major Arjun's prowess as a soldier and his unwavering determination inspired his fellow officers to fight with unmatched ferocity.

Hours passed, and the situation gradually began to favor the Indian Army. The terrorists, caught off guard by the Army's relentless assault, started to retreat. Major Arjun, however, knew the battle wasn't over yet. He sensed that the enemy's retreat was merely a ploy to regroup and launch a counter-offensive.

Anticipating this, Major Arjun and his team swiftly moved to secure and fortify their position. They were not going to let the enemy slip away and endanger their lives once more. Their vigilance paid off, as the terrorists soon launched a desperate attack.

Major Arjun's team valiantly held the line, their determination unwavering and their hearts filled with the knowledge that they were fighting for each other, for their fallen comrades, and for the honor of the Indian Army.

As the battle raged on, Major Arjun, with his astute tactical skills, neutralized the enemy's leader, effectively disheartening the terrorists and shattering their morale. With their defense crumbling, the remaining terrorists fled, leaving behind their weapons and equipment.

The battle had been won, and the lives of Captain Vikram and the other officers were saved. Major Arjun's heroic leadership and unwavering commitment had been the key to their miraculous escape from the clutches of death.

News of Major Arjun's bravery spread like wildfire, and he was hailed as a true hero. But for him, the only reward that mattered was the renewed strength and camaraderie among the surviving officers. For their lives were forever connected, bonded by the indomitable spirit of brotherhood forged on the battlefield.

From that day forward, Major Arjun continued to serve with honor and distinction, inspiring others with his selfless acts of valor and unwavering commitment to the Indian Army. And Captain Vikram, forever grateful to his friend and savior, followed in his footsteps, determined to uphold the legacy of bravery and brotherhood that Major Arjun had exemplified.

A Sniper - Relentless Pursuit of Peace

In the rugged terrains of the Kashmir Valley, Captain Vikram Singh, an Indian Army sniper, took position on a hilltop overlooking a militant camp. After a month of relentless pursuit, the intelligence had lead him to this moment, where victory stood precariously on the tip of his rifle.

As the sun dipped below the horizon, the valley fell silent, engulfing Captain Singh in an eerie stillness. He adjusted his scope, focused his gaze, and let the weight of his duty settle on his shoulders. For him, it was not just the lives of his comrades at stake, but the hopes of a nation desperate for peace.

Through the camouflage of darkness, Captain Singh studied the camp, assessing his targets. He was aware that beyond the enemy combatants lay a web of intricate choices - choices that had brought him here, choices that threatened to consume him during the never-ending nights.

A sudden flare of gunfire jolted Captain Singh from his thoughts. The militants, apparently suspecting an attack, were exchanging fire with an Indian platoon a few kilometers away. Captain Singh knew it was his moment to strike, to unleash the fury of a sniper trained in precision and valor.

With steady hands and unwavering determination, he positioned his finger on the trigger. Hesitation and doubt were not part of his repertoire; his mission was clear and stakes higher than ever. The clock ticked as he calculated the bullet trajectory and anticipated the wind speed. Every move had to be perfect, or else the fragile chance for victory could slip away.

One by one, Captain Singh's bullets transformed into silent justice, eliminating the enemy and reducing their numbers. The militants struggled to comprehend the invisible wrath that was raining down upon them. The captain's relentless assault sent waves of fear through their ranks, causing chaos and disarray.

Amidst the chaos, Captain Singh noticed a young militant trying to flee. A wave of empathy washed over him, desperate to save a life ensnared by the clutches of extremism. In that fleeting moment, he considered sparing the youth. However, the reality of the situation crashed over him. He had to make a choice - sacrifice potential compassion for the greater good of his mission.

With a heavy heart, he took aim. A split second passed, and the bullet gracefully soared through the air, meeting its intended target. The young militant's lifeless body crumbled, reducing Captain Singh's heart to ash. Victory, it seemed, required sacrifice - even the sacrifice of compassion.

As the final echoes of gunfire faded into the night, Captain Singh surveyed the aftermath of his triumphant mission. The once-avid militants now lay defeated and silenced. Yet, within his victory, he found no solace, no celebration. Instead, he was burdened with the weight of the sacrifices incurred, both by the enemy and his own conscience.

As the sun began to rise over the Kashmir Valley, Captain Singh retreated from his position, carrying with him not only the deafening silence of his accomplishment but also the scars of his choices. With each step, he understood that victory for an army sniper was not merely in the elimination of enemies but in the relentless pursuit of peace, even if it cost him his own humanity.

AFGHANISTAN - Resilience and Strength of the Human Spirit.

Rajesh Kumar had left his comfortable life in India to work as an engineer for a construction project in Afghanistan. He never anticipated that his skills and determination would be put to the ultimate test - fighting the Taliban to protect a pregnant woman.

While the world mostly associated Afghanistan with conflict and turmoil, Rajesh believed that his work could make a difference, bringing stability and progress to the war-torn nation. Little did he know that his personal convictions would soon be put to the ultimate test.

One hot summer day, as Rajesh was supervising the construction site, he noticed a commotion nearby. Curiosity got the better of him, and he heard the cries of a woman in distress. Pushing through the crowd, he found himself standing at the entrance of a small shop.

Inside, he saw a terrified young woman, Fatima, who was heavily pregnant. The Taliban militants had barged into the shop, demanding that she reveal the whereabouts of her husband, who they believed was a spy. Rajesh's heart went out to Fatima, and in that moment, he made a silent vow to protect her and her unborn child.

Without hesitation, Rajesh took matters into his own hands. He swiftly fabricated a story, presenting Fatima as his own wife who was suffering from a rare medical condition. His acting skills had never been put to the test before, but he couldn't afford even the slightest mistake. He begged the Taliban soldiers for mercy, desperately pleading for her safety.

To Rajesh's surprise, his acting skills proved fruitful. The Taliban, intrigued by this sudden twist, decided to spare Fatima and instructed her to leave the city immediately. However, they warned Rajesh not to deceive them, as they would be watching him closely.

Rajesh knew that simply hiding Fatima would never be enough to ensure her safety. He devised a plan to smuggle her to a nearby village, known for its resistance against the Taliban. Gathering some of the locals who were sympathetic to their cause, Rajesh and Fatima embarked on a perilous journey.

For weeks, they evaded Taliban checkpoints, braving treacherous terrains and staying hidden during the day. Rajesh's engineering skills proved instrumental in their survival, as he devised clever hiding places and makeshift shelters along the way.

Eventually, they reached the village, where they found sanctuary among the brave men and women who had been fighting against the Taliban. Rajesh's determination to protect Fatima had not only saved her and her unborn child but had also inspired others to stand against the tyranny of the Taliban.

Rajesh's act of bravery had not gone unnoticed. News of his courageous escape quickly spread, and he became a symbol of hope for many. The Indian expat had inadvertently become a hero in a foreign land, fighting for the rights and safety of the Afghan people.

As the years rolled by, Rajesh continued his work in Afghanistan. The construction project he had taken on became more than just his job; it became his mission to rebuild not only the physical infrastructure but also the lives shattered by conflict. His tale served as a reminder that one man's dedication and sacrifice can ignite a fire of change.

Rajesh's story was eventually captured by journalists, who shared it with the world, shedding light on the trials faced by the Afghan people. His determination to protect Fatima had become a testament to the resilience and strength of the human spirit.

The struggles and triumphs of Rajesh and Fatima served as an inspiration to countless others, proving that sometimes, in the darkest of times, ordinary people can rise to become heroes and protectors. Their story became a beacon of hope for those who had lost faith, reminding them that the fight for justice and freedom was worth every sacrifice.

Sikhs - The Protectors

In the bustling city of London, a group of four Sikh men found themselves united by a common purpose - to bridge the gap of misunderstanding and protect their Muslim brothers and sisters from the repercussions of hatred borne out of the actions of a few misguided individuals. Deep-rooted in their Sikh faith, which teaches equality and compassion for all, they stood tall as beacons of hope in these troubled times.

Word had spread quickly about a planned protest outside a local mosque, spurred on by anger and fear after yet another act of terrorism committed by extremists. But these four Sikhs, each coming from different walks of life, had etched out a bond that transcended religious differences.

Gurdeep, an esteemed lawyer with a fearless demeanor, spearheaded the group's efforts to protect the mosque. Balwinder, a humble shop owner with a heart of gold, opened his store as a meeting place for strategizing and coordination. Rajdeep, a tech-savvy Sikh who used his skills to gather information, provided valuable insights on the protest's scale and the potential threat it posed. And lastly, Jasminder, a tall and robust man who had dedicated his life to martial arts, stood as the group's physical shield.

With conviction burning in their hearts, the four Sikhs meticulously developed a plan to safeguard the mosque and its worshippers. They knew they were treading on a delicate line, balancing between their desire to protect their Muslim community and the necessity to defuse the volatile situation.

On the day of the protest, as dawn settled over the city, the four Sikhs positioned themselves in strategic locations around the mosque. Gurdeep, dressed sharply in a suit, took up a position near the entrance, ready to address any legal concerns and mediate discussions. Balwinder, gentle yet resolute, stood by the protest organizers, armed with calmness and a genuine willingness to engage in dialogue.

Rajdeep, donning a jacket with hidden pockets concealing his technological tools, observed the overall atmosphere, his focus on potential threats from the sidelines. And Jasminder, an imposing figure with a turban and flowing beard, positioned himself near the mosque's gate, radiating strength and determination to protect those inside.

As the day progressed, emotions flared, and tensions began to rise. Protesters shouted slogans and waved angry banners, but the presence of the four Sikhs served as a stark contrast to the hate-filled atmosphere. Their stoic resilience and unwavering commitment to peace commanded respect, sowing the seeds of doubt in the minds of those who had come fueled by anger.

Gurdeep initiated conversations, engaging in calm discussions with individuals willing to listen. He empathized with their concerns, while showcasing the teachings of Sikhism that echo the values of love, unity, and equality. Balwinder, with his soft-spoken nature, managed to find common ground with some of the protest organizers, reminding them of the importance of unity amongst diverse communities.

As time wore on, the atmosphere started to shift. A few protesters, intrigued by the Sikhs' display of solidarity, cautiously approached Rajdeep, seeking to understand their motives. Rajdeep, seizing the opportunity, used his skills to access information on the tragic past the Sikh community shared with Muslims during the Partition of India. He recounted stories of camaraderie and protection that had been extended to the Muslim community during those dark times, emphasizing the importance of unity against a shared enemy - hatred.

Meanwhile, Jasminder's towering presence and calm demeanor had a tranquilizing effect on both mosque-goers and protesters alike. The mere sight of him, guarding the entrance with grace and compassion, disarmed individuals harboring prejudice and provided solace to those seeking refuge within the mosque's walls.

The evening drew closer, and the once-fiery protest had transformed into a platform for dialogue and understanding. The passage of time, coupled with the unwavering efforts of these four Sikhs, had managed to sow seeds of compassion amidst the chaos. A handful of protesters cautiously entered the mosque to engage in conversation, acknowledging the importance of standing together against extremism.

Days turned into weeks, and the impact of the four Sikhs' actions reverberated throughout London. Their solidarity had become a symbol of hope, inspiring others to follow suit and protect their fellow humans, regardless of religious affiliation. The protests had transformed into community discussions, fostering empathy and learning among different faiths.

In the end, this tale showcased the triumph of unity over division. These four Sikhs had shown the world that love can prevail, even in the face of adversity. Their unwavering commitment had bridged divides, altering the course of hate and bringing about an understanding that no religion could be held accountable for the actions of a few.

London became a city known for its unity, strength, and the resilience of its diverse community. And amidst it all, the mosque stood as a beacon of hope, its doors open to all, forever.

COVID 19 - Saviour becomes Friend for LIFE!!!

In the bustling city of Jaipur, the scorching sun beat down on the streets, casting long shadows over the vibrant buildings. The air was thick with tension and fear, as the city battled against the relentless spread of the COVID-19 pandemic. In the midst of this chaos, an Indian stranger stepped into the scene, his face masked and his heart full of compassion.

Rajesh, a middle-aged man, had arrived in Jaipur a few months ago for a business venture. Little did he know that his life was about to take an unexpected turn. One morning, as he walked down the street, he noticed a frail woman lying on the pavement, struggling to catch her breath. Her eyes were filled with fear and helplessness.

Filled with concern, Rajesh approached her and offered his assistance. Despite the language barrier, he managed to convey his sincerity through gestures and kind words. Realizing the gravity of the situation, Rajesh gently lifted the woman and carried her to the nearby hospital.

Upon reaching, Rajesh learned that the woman, named Meera, had contracted the deadly virus. Her condition was critical, and she needed immediate medical attention. However, the overburdened healthcare system struggled to provide adequate care for all the patients flooding in.

Driven by compassion, Rajesh refused to leave Meera's side, vowing to do everything in his power to help her survive this battle. He started by speaking to doctors, advocating for her care and ensuring she received the necessary treatment. Whenever possible, he would sit beside Meera, holding her hand and offering words of comfort. He understood the power of hope, and he was determined to instill it within her.

Days turned into weeks, and Meera's condition gradually improved, thanks to the relentless efforts of the medical staff and Rajesh's unwavering support. As she regained her strength, she began to open up to Rajesh, sharing her fears, dreams, and the struggles she faced as a single mother in this unforgiving city.

Rajesh, moved by Meera's resilience and determination, decided to take matters into his own hands. He reached out to his extensive network of friends and colleagues, seeking financial assistance to help Meera rebuild her life once she recovered. The response was overwhelming, with many eager to contribute to her cause.

With the funds raised, Rajesh arranged for a small apartment for Meera and her daughter, ensuring they had a safe and comfortable place to call home. He also arranged for Meera's daughter to be enrolled in a reputable school, promising her a brighter future.

Months passed, and the city of Jaipur began to heal. Rajesh and Meera's bond grew stronger, their friendship evolving into a true family connection. They stood as a testament to the power of kindness and compassion, reminding the world that in times of darkness, selfless acts of love can restore hope.

As news of their heart warming journey spread throughout the city, Rajesh became an inspiration to others, encouraging everyone to stand together and help those in need. His actions ignited a flame of unity, bringing the community closer, and reminding them that they could overcome any challenge through compassion and support.

In a city burdened by fear and uncertainty, an Indian stranger had stepped forward, transforming lives and reminding everyone of the remarkable strength of the human spirit. And amidst the chaos, the city of Jaipur became a beacon of hope, shining brightly in the face of adversity.

Heroes need not be Humans only

Once upon a time, in a quiet suburban neighborhood, there lived a family with a beloved pet dog named Max. Max was a gentle and loyal Golden Retriever known for his friendly demeanor and playful nature. The family treated Max as one of their own, showering him with love and affection. Little did they know that Max's loyalty would one day be put to the ultimate test.

In the same neighborhood, a group of heartless kidnappers had been operating in secret. Their sinister activities sent shivers down the spines of the unsuspecting residents. They targeted vulnerable families, choosing their victims carefully. One afternoon, as fate would have it, they set their sights on a family with a newborn infant.

As the parents attended to their daily chores, little did they know that danger was lurking just outside their home. The kidnappers cunningly observed the family's routines, seeking the perfect moment to strike. They planned to snatch the baby while the parents were briefly occupied.

Unbeknownst to the kidnappers, Max had sensed their malevolent intentions. He had noticed their suspicious presence in the neighborhood and could feel their evil intentions in the air. Unyielding in his duty to protect his family, Max kept a watchful eye on the surroundings.

On that fateful afternoon, as the parents took a momentary break from their tasks, the kidnappers seized the opportunity. Silently, they entered the house, their malevolent smiles concealed beneath their sinister masks. The house was filled with an eerie silence as they made their way to the nursery, where the infant was gently sleeping.

Max, however, was not far behind. He had been quietly following their every move from a distance. As the kidnappers approached the nursery, Max's bark rang out in the house, ferocious and resolute. Instantly, the parents' hearts skipped a beat as they hurriedly rushed towards the room.

The kidnappers froze in their tracks, startled by the unexpected resistance they encountered. Max, fueled by his love for his family, stood valiantly between them and the innocent baby. His eyes gleamed with fierce determination, his teeth bared, ready to defend.

The kidnappers, realizing their plan had been foiled, saw no other choice but to retreat. Fleeing in fear, they left the house just as quickly as they had entered it. They never dared to return to that neighborhood again.

The family, forever grateful for Max's bravery, showered him with heartfelt affection. He had defied all odds and potentially saved their child from falling victim to those wicked individuals. Max had proven that his love and loyalty knew no bounds.

Word of Max's heroic act soon spread throughout the neighbourhood, earning him the status of a local hero. People admired his selfless act of protection and showcased their love and appreciation for him. Max, however, remained humble, content in knowing his family was safe.

From that day forward, Max became known as the guardian angel of the neighbourhood. Residents felt a sense of security, knowing that their trusty four-legged friend was always watching over them. Max's legacy of bravery and loyalty would forever be remembered, proving that sometimes, the most powerful heroes are the ones who walk on four legs and wag their tails.

Light at the End of the Tunnel

Once a bustling hive of activity and a symbol of New York City's strength and resilience, the Twin Towers now lay in ruins, a painful reminder of the horrific events that took place on September 11th, 2001. Among the heroes that day was Fireman Michael Sullivan, who bravely entered the towers to evacuate as many people as possible before they collapsed. Little did he know that this would be just the beginning of his journey.

As the dust settled and the city mourned, Michael found himself haunted by the images and sounds of that fateful day. The echoes of screams and the cries for help followed him like a relentless shadow, invading his thoughts day and night. The weight of survivor's guilt weighed heavily on his shoulders, as he questioned if there was something more he could have done. He couldn't shake off the feeling that he had let someone down, even though he knew he had done all he could.

To seek solace and healing, Michael made the decision to embark on a road trip across America. With a small trailer hitched to the back of his truck, he set off on a journey of self-discovery, hoping to find peace within himself and make sense of the tragedy.

His first stop was in a small town in Pennsylvania, where he met a young girl named Emily. She had lost her father on 9/11, and the two instantly formed a deep connection. As they shared their stories of loss and survival, Michael found comfort in knowing that he was not alone in his grief. Together, they visited the Flight 93 National Memorial, paying tribute to the heroes who thwarted another potential catastrophe that day.

Continuing his journey, Michael arrived in Oklahoma City. There, he visited the Oklahoma City National Memorial, a place that reminded him of the resilience of a community that had also faced tragedy. He met survivors, listened to their stories, and learned that healing is a collective effort.

Further west, Michael found himself in New Mexico, where he stumbled upon a wildfire threatening a small town. Without hesitation, he joined the local fire department in their battle against the flames. As he fought desperately to save lives and homes, a realization struck him – just as he had valiantly fought to save lives in the Twin Towers, this time he was also finding purpose and redemption through his actions.

Word of Michael's valiant efforts spread, and before he knew it, he became a symbol of resilience, hope, and the unwavering spirit of a nation. Communities across America began celebrating him as not just a hero of 9/11 but also as a hero who continued to serve. Fire departments invited him to speak at their events, schools requested him to share his story with their students, and he became an advocate for mental health support for first responders.

The journey not only helped Michael find solace but also provided him with a newfound purpose. As he traversed the country, he realized that the gratitude and recognition he received were not just for him but for all the heroes who had risked their lives on 9/11. It was their collective sacrifice, their unwavering courage that had shaped the nation and its response to tragedy.

On the anniversary of 9/11, Michael found himself back in New York City, standing where the Twin Towers once stood tall. As he looked at the rebuilt World Trade Center, he felt a surge of hope and resilience. The journey had transformed him, reminding him of the strength that can arise from even the darkest of moments.

With tears in his eyes, Michael whispered a silent thank you to all those who perished that day, vowing to carry their memory in his heart forever. He knew he couldn't change the past, but he had found his purpose in helping others heal and in honouring the courage displayed on that tragic day in September.

And so, Fireman Michael Sullivan continued to travel the country, telling his story, while offering support and love to those affected by the WTC massacre, and reminding them that even in the aftermath of unspeakable tragedy, there is always hope.

The Jungle King

In the remote and dense jungles of India, where the echoes of war had long been forgotten, a group of terrorists plotted their nefarious plans. Under the moonlit sky, they strategized their ambush, hoping to strike fear into the hearts of the innocent. Little did they know, the brave soldiers of the Indian army were always one step ahead, prepared to face any challenge that crossed their path.

The morning sun rose, casting its golden glow upon the rolling hills and lush greenery. Deep within the heart of the jungle, a battalion of elite Indian army soldiers set out on a routine patrol. Their determination and unwavering courage was their shield against the unseen enemy.

As they cautiously navigated through the dense foliage, the soldiers felt the eyes of the terrorists watching their every move. They pressed forward, their senses sharpened, prepared for any danger.

Unbeknownst to the terrorists, Lieutenant Vikram Singh, an extraordinary soldier with extraordinary instincts, sensed the presence of danger. As the soldiers continued trudging through the jungle, Vikram discreetly signaled his comrades to take cover. He knew that the trap had been set.

Within moments, gunfire erupted from all directions as the terrorists launched their ambush. The peaceful forest transformed into a chaotic battlefield, with bullets whizzing through the air and smoke billowing from the muzzles of guns.

Vikram and his comrades fought back with unwavering determination, their training and experience guiding their every move. They moved with precision, skillfully navigating the changing landscape of danger and adversity. As fiery explosions reverberated through the trees, the Indian soldiers remained resolute, their unwavering patriotism shining through the darkest of moments.

Amidst the chaos, a defining moment came when Vikram spotted the enemy leader, Khalid, leading the charge. Khalid was notorious for his ruthlessness and his desire to instill fear in the hearts of the innocent. With a spirit aflame, Vikram focused his attention on bringing down this ruthless man, who had caused so much pain and suffering.

Ignoring the chaos around him, Vikram closed in on Khalid, his heartbeat racing with a mix of anticipation and determination. The two adversaries locked eyes for a brief moment before the battle resumed. They fought fiercely, each move calculated and met with equal ferocity. The forest bore witness to the intensity of their struggle, as the clash of steel and the echo of gunshots filled the air.

Finally, after what felt like an eternity, Vikram seized an opportunity. With a swift maneuver, he disarmed Khalid, leaving him at his mercy. His gaze steady and unwavering, Vikram spoke with a voice that carried the weight of justice. "Your reign of terror ends here, Khalid."

The sound of gunfire quieted as the remaining terrorists, realizing their leader's defeat, surrendered to the Indian soldiers. With the ambush thwarted and the threat neutralized, the calmness of peace was restored to the jungle.

Vikram's bravery and leadership were celebrated, bringing hope to the hearts of his comrades and the people they served. The story of their triumph would forever be etched in the annals of Indian military history.

In the aftermath of the ambush, the Indian army stood tall, a beacon of strength and resilience. They remained vigilant, protectors of the innocent, ready to face any obstacle that threatened the peace of their beloved nation. And in every dark corner of the world, the defeated terrorists would remember the unwavering heroes who had triumphed against the odds, embodying the spirit of bravery and sacrifice.

Echoes of Valour

Once upon a time in the mountainous region of Kargil, situated in the breathtaking backdrop of the Himalayas, a war was fought that would forever etch itself into the annals of history. It was the summer of 1999, and tensions between neighboring nations had reached a boiling point. India and Pakistan stood locked in a bitter conflict that would come to be known as the Kargil War.

In the quaint village of Dras, far away from the bustling cities, a young boy named Arjun grew up surrounded by tales of valor and sacrifice. His grandfather, a retired soldier, would often regale him with stories of heroes who fought with unwavering determination to protect their homeland. These stories ignited a deep sense of patriotism within Arjun's heart and ignited a burning desire to make a difference.

As he grew older, the turbulent years leading up to the Kargil War began to unfold before his eyes. The news spoke of mortars raining down upon the land of Kargil, of brave soldiers scaling treacherous peaks, and courageous pilots flying above uncharted territory. The war had become a reality, a harsh reality that would determine the fate of the nation.

One morning, as Arjun gazed at the peaks that loomed above his village, he made a decision that would change his life. Determined to fight for his country, he enlisted in the Indian Army. It was not an easy path, but Arjun was filled with an indomitable spirit and an unyielding resolve to face any challenge that lay ahead.

Training was grueling, pushing him to his limits physically and mentally. Yet, Arjun persevered, drawing strength from the stories his grandfather had shared with him. He learned the art of warfare, the importance of unity, and the value of discipline. With each passing day, he grew closer to becoming a soldier, a warrior clad in the uniform that symbolized sacrifice and honor.

The day finally arrived when Arjun found himself on the frontlines of the battlefield. The majestic mountains of Kargil stood tall and proud, their peaks echoing the thunderous clashes that filled the air. He and his comrades took solemn vows to protect their homeland with their very lives if necessary.

In the darkness of the night, under the gaze of the moon, Arjun and his fellow soldiers commenced their mission to reclaim the peaks that had been captured by the enemy. It was a dangerous endeavor, fraught with peril, but their unwavering determination and strategic brilliance pushed them forward.

Days turned into weeks, and with each passing day, Arjun faced the horrors of war head-on. He witnessed the futility of violence, the tragedies of loss, and the unbreakable bond that formed among his comrades. Through the fury of battle, he discovered what true courage meant - not the absence of fear, but rather the willingness to face it, overcoming it for a greater cause.

As the war raged on, Arjun's valor and leadership on the battlefield became renowned. He was recognized as a brave soldier, leading his men with unwavering determination in the face of unimaginable odds. Their unity, skill, and unrelenting spirit turned the tides of the war, inch by inch, peak by peak.

Finally, after months of grueling battle, victory was achieved. The peaks of Kargil had been reclaimed, and the Indian flag once again stood atop the mountains that had witnessed the bravery of countless heroes. Arjun's heart swelled with pride as he looked upon the land that he and his comrades had fought so fiercely to defend.

The echoes of the Kargil War reverberated throughout history, reminding future generations of the bravery, sacrifices, and indomitable spirit of those who had fought for their nation. And within those echoes, the story of Arjun, a young boy who had grown into a fearless warrior, who had risen above adversity to leave an indelible mark of his own, would forever be cherished.

The Battle of Kurukshetra

The Battle of Kurukshetra was a legendary event that took place thousands of years ago in the ancient land of India. It was a battle that changed the course of history, leaving a lasting impact on the lives of those who participated.

The story begins with two mighty warrior clans, the Pandavas and the Kauravas, locked in a bitter feud over the rightful claim to the throne. The Pandavas, led by the virtuous Yudhishthira, were righteous and just, while the Kauravas, led by the malicious Duryodhana, were driven by greed and envy.

As the tension grew, it became clear that the battle was inevitable. The Pandavas, aware of the dire consequences of war, tried to find a peaceful solution to avoid bloodshed, but the Kauravas remained steadfast in their desire for power. The kingdom was divided, and war became the only path to resolution.

The battlefield of Kurukshetra was vast, stretching for miles with its fertile land and gentle winds. The armies, numbering in the millions on each side, gathered on either end of this hallowed ground, their spirits charged and their eagerness to prove their mettle visible in their eyes.

At the breaking of dawn, the conch shells of warriors echoed through the air, as the opposing forces blew them to signal the start of the battle. Mighty chariots collided, arrows soared through the sky, and blood stained the once-pristine land. The clashing of weapons drowned out all other sounds as warriors from both sides fought fiercely, fuelled by their determination to emerge victorious.

In the midst of it all, Arjuna, the skilled archer and Pandava prince, found himself overwhelmed by the sight of his own relatives fighting for the side of evil. Confused and disheartened, he turned to his charioteer, Lord Krishna, who was an incarnation of the divine.

Arjuna poured out his heart to Krishna, devastated by the thought of harming those who were dear to him. Addressing his despair, Krishna began to impart words of wisdom, guiding Arjuna towards his duty, reminding him that this battle was not just about victory or defeat, but about righteousness prevailing over evil.

Arjuna listened attentively to each word, his spirit rekindled with a newfound understanding. With renewed determination, he picked up his bow and arrow, taking his place at the forefront of the battlefield. The Pandavas, inspired by his resilience, rallied and fought with a renewed vigor.

Days turned into nights, and the battle raged on relentlessly. Both sides suffered heavy casualties, their grief and pain etched in their eyes but still, they fought on. In those moments of chaos and destruction, heroes and legends were born, their bravery eternally remembered.

Finally, after eighteen grueling days, the Battle of Kurukshetra came to an end. The Pandavas emerged victorious, their unwavering righteousness prevailing over the Kauravas' malevolence. The battlefield was strewn with the fallen, a poignant reminder of the cost of war.

Through this epic battle, the world witnessed the power of duty, the strength of moral values, and the consequences of blinding hunger for power. The Battle of Kurukshetra became a timeless tale, teaching generations about the importance of righteousness and the devastating effects of greed.

The story of Kurukshetra remains etched in the annals of history, reminding humanity that even in the darkest of times, there is always hope for justice and righteousness to prevail.

The Warrior Prince

Long ago, in the ancient kingdom of Hastinapura, there lived a mighty warrior prince named Karna. Born to a humble mother and abandoned by his royal father, Karna faced a childhood filled with hardships and struggles. Yet, he grew up to become a man of unparalleled strength, skill, and honor, known throughout the lands for his unwavering loyalty and indomitable spirit.

Karna possessed remarkable archery skills, which rivalled even the greatest archers of his time. However, fate dealt him an unfortunate hand, and his noble origins remained a secret, hidden from the world. Despite this, Karna never allowed his circumstances to define him. Instead, he forged his own destiny through his unwavering determination and unrelenting bravery.

Known for his integrity, Karna garnered the respect and admiration of many, including Duryodhana, the ambitious prince of the Kuru dynasty. Duryodhana recognized Karna's immense talent and unwavering loyalty, and he embraced him as an equal, seeing in Karna a true friend.

As the kingdom of Hastinapura faced impending war, Duryodhana sought alliances from all corners of the realm. Karna, standing firmly by his friend, pledged his unwavering support, even when others doubted Duryodhana's intentions. Karna's steadfast loyalty was not swayed by politics or power; he stood by Duryodhana because he believed in his friend, valuing their bond above all else.

The war, known as the Kurukshetra war, arrived, and Karna unleashed his fury upon the battlefield with unmatched ferocity. In every encounter, he displayed remarkable skills and undefeated valor, leading his army into numerous victories. However, despite his unmatched prowess, the weight of his destiny began to weigh heavily upon his shoulders.

Krishna, the divine charioteer of his half-brother Arjuna, recognized Karna's true heritage and sought to reveal it to him. Krishna understood that Karna's real strength lay not only in his physical abilities but also in the moral choices he made. Thus, he approached Karna, revealing his true identity as the son of the Sun God and his royal lineage as the half-brother of Arjuna.

Overwhelmed by this revelation, Karna wrestled with conflicting emotions. On one hand, he felt the weight of his loyalty towards Duryodhana, who had embraced him when no one else would. On the other hand, he felt the longing to embrace his true destiny and reunite with his brothers, the Pandavas.

As the war raged on, the pivotal moment arrived when Karna faced Arjuna, his true brother, on the battlefield. Karna was torn between fulfilling his duty as Duryodhana's loyal friend and honoring his newfound identity as a prince of the Pandava dynasty. In that moment of dilemma, Karna made a life-altering decision.

Despite his love for Duryodhana, Karna laid down his weapons, unable to raise his bow against his brothers. He revealed his true identity to everyone, including Duryodhana, who was stunned by the profound sacrifice Karna was willing to make for his honor.

The battlefield fell silent as a newfound respect for Karna emanated from all sides. Even Arjuna, Karna's greatest rival, recognized the noble spirit within him. In a gesture of utmost reverence, Arjuna saluted Karna, acknowledging his integrity and unwavering loyalty.

With his head held high, Karna put honor above victory and integrity above loyalty. He had made his choice and lived by his principles till the very end. He had become more than a warrior prince; he was an embodiment of character and virtue.

Though Karna did not survive the war, his legend persisted throughout time. His story became a symbol of courage, sacrifice, and loyalty. Karna, the warrior prince who remained true to his principles, would forever be remembered as the epitome of honor and integrity, inspiring generations to come.